Good-bye,
382 Shin Dang Dong

Frances Park and Ginger Park

Illustrated by Yangsook Choi

NATIONAL
GEOGRAPHIC
WASHINGTON, D.C.

To our parents, Sei-Young and Heisook Park,

and to Phil and Ada Nogee,

our parents' first friends on Foster Terrace.

—FP AND GP

For my friend, Kitae Kim.

—YC

My heart beats in two places: Here, where I live, and also in a place where I once lived. You see, I was born in Korea. One day my parents told me we were moving to America. I was eight years old, old enough to keep many lovely memories of my birthplace alive in my heart forever. But one very sad memory stays with me, too. The day I cried, "Good-bye, 382 Shin Dang Dong!"

O*n that summer day* I woke up to the sound of light rain tapping on my window. The monsoon season was coming. I didn't even need to open my eyes to know that. It was that time of year. It was also time to move.

In a few hours, I would be on an airplane.

When I opened my eyes, my heart sank. My bedroom was so bare! No hand-painted scrolls or colorful fans on my walls. No silk cushions or straw mats on my floor. All my possessions were packed away in a big brown box marked "Lovely Things."

I frowned and listened to the raindrops. One, two, three... Soon the thick of the monsoon would arrive, and a thousand raindrops would hit our clay-tiled roof all at once. But I wouldn't be here to listen to them. I would be halfway around the world in a strange, foreign place called 112 Foster Terrace, Brighton, Massachusetts, U.S.A.

My parents were very excited.

"Jangmi, you will like America," Dad tried to assure me.

"Are the seasons the same?" I wondered.

"Oh, yes."

"With monsoon rains."

"No, Jangmi, no monsoon rains."

"No friends either," I moaned.

"You will make many new friends in America," Mom promised me, "in your new home."

But I loved my home right here! I didn't want to go to America and make new friends. I didn't want to leave my best friend, Kisuni.

After breakfast, Kisuni and I ran out into the rain and to the open market. Monsoon season was also the season for sweet, yellow melons called *chummy.* Kisuni and I would often peel and eat chummy under the willow tree that stood outside my bedroom window. But today, the chummy were for guests who were coming over for a farewell lunch.

At the market we peered into endless baskets and took our time choosing the ripest, plumpest chummy we could find.

"Do they have chummy in America?" Kisuni wondered.

"No," I replied. "But my mom says they have melons called honeydew."

"Honeydew," Kisuni giggled. "What a funny name!"

Soon after we returned, family and friends began to arrive, carrying pots and plates of food. One by one they took off their shoes, then entered the house. Grandmother was dressed in her most special occasion *hanbok.* She set up the long *bap sang* and before I could even blink, on it were a big pot of dumpling soup and the prettiest pastel rice cakes I had ever seen. Kisuni and I peeled and sliced our chummy and carefully arranged the pieces on a plate.

Then everybody ate and sang traditional Korean songs and celebrated in a sad way. Love and laughter and tears rippled through our house. How I wanted to pack these moments into a big brown box and bring them with me to America.

Kisuni and I sneaked outside and sat beneath the willow tree. We watched the rain with glum faces.

"Kisuni, I wish we never had to move from this spot," I said.

"Me, too," she sighed. "Jangmi, how far away is America?"

"My mom says that it's halfway around the world. And my dad told me that when the moon is shining here, the sun is shining there. That's how far apart we'll be," I moaned.

"That's really far," Kisuni moaned back.

We watched the rain and grew more glum than ever. Then Kisuni perked up.

"So when you're awake, I'll be asleep. And when I'm awake, you'll be asleep," she declared. "At least we'll always know what the other one is doing."

That moment our faces brightened. But a moment later we had to say good-bye.

Kisuni held back her tears. "Promise you'll write to me, Jangmi."

"I promise, Kisuni."

It was time to go to the airport.

"Kimpo Airport," Dad instructed the taxi driver.

The taxi slowly pulled away. I looked at our beautiful home one last time. Like rain on the window, tears streaked down my face.

"Good-bye, 382 Shin Dang Dong!" I cried.

On the long ride to the airport, Dad asked me, "Do you want to know what your new home looks like?"

"Okay," I shrugged.

"Let's see," Dad began, "it's a row house."

"A house that's attached to other houses," Mom explained.

"And inside the house are wooden floors," Dad added.

"No *ondal* floors?" I asked him. "How will we keep warm in the winter without ondal floors?"

"There are radiators in every room!" Mom said with an enthusiastic clap. "And a fireplace in the living room! Imagine!"

No, I could not imagine that. In our home we had a fire in the cellar called the ondal. It stayed lit all the time. The heat from the ondal traveled through underground pipes and kept our wax-covered floors warm and cozy. A fireplace in the living room sounded peculiar to me.

"And the rooms are separated by wooden doors," Mom added.

"No rice paper doors?" I wondered.

My parents shook their heads. "No, Jangmi."

My eyes closed with disappointment. I had a hard time picturing this house. Would it ever feel like home?

On the airplane, I sat by the window. We flew over rice fields and clay-tiled roofs. Already I felt homesick.

The next thing I knew we were flying over the ocean. At first I could see fishing boats rocking in the waters. As we climbed higher into the clouds, the boats grew smaller and smaller. Suddenly, the world looked very big to me.

"Good-bye, 382 Shin Dang Dong," I cried again.

Dad sat back in his seat and began to read an American newspaper. The words were all foreign.

"Dad," I asked, "how will I ever learn to understand English?"

"It's not so hard," he said. "Would you like to learn an English word?"

"Okay," I sighed.

After a pause, Dad came up with —

"Rose."

"Rose?" I repeated. "What does that mean?"

"That's the English translation of your Korean name," Mom said.

"Rose means Jangmi?" I asked.

"Yes," my parents nodded.

"Rose," I said over and over.

"Would you like to adopt Rose as your American name?" Mom asked me.

"No, I like *my* name," I insisted.

On a foggy morning four days later, we arrived in Massachusetts. After we gathered our luggage, we climbed into an airport taxi.

Even through the fog, I could see that things were very different in America. There were big, wide roads called highways. The rooftops were shingled instead of clay-tiled. People shopped in glass-enclosed stores instead of open markets. No rice fields, no monsoon rains. So many foreign faces.

Slowly, the taxi pulled up to a row house on a quiet street. Red brick steps led up to a wooden door.

"Here we are, Jangmi," Dad said, "112 Foster Terrace, Brighton, Massachusetts, U.S.A."

The house was just as my parents had described. I took off my shoes and walked on wooden floors. They felt very cold. I opened wooden doors. They felt very heavy. Outside, the fog had lifted. But inside, everything felt dark and strange.

"Look," Dad pointed out the window, "there's a tree just like the one at home."

"No, it's not, Dad. It's not a willow tree," I said.

"No," he agreed. "It's a maple tree. But isn't it beautiful?"

382 Shin Dang Dong, 382 Shin Dang Dong. I wanted to go home to 382 Shin Dang Dong right now. Only a knock at the door saved me from tears.

Mom announced, "The movers are here!"

The house quickly filled up with furniture and big brown boxes. The box marked "Lovely Things" was the last to arrive.

I unpacked all my possessions. I hung my hand-painted scrolls and colorful fans on the walls. I placed my silk cushions and straw mats on the floor.

Then came another knock. To our surprise a parade of neighbors waltzed in carrying plates of curious food. There were pink-and-white iced cakes and warm pans containing something called casseroles.

A girl my age wandered up to me with a small glass bowl. Inside the bowl were colorful balls. They smelled fruity.

She pointed to a red ball and said, "Watermelon!" She pointed to an orange ball and said, "Cantaloupe!" Lastly she pointed to a green ball and said, "Honeydew!"

I took a green ball and tasted it. Mmm… it was as sweet and delicious as chummy.

The girl asked me a question. But I couldn't understand her.

"She wants to know what kind of fruit you eat in Korea," Dad stepped in.

"Chummy," I replied.

"Chummy," the girl repeated, then giggled—just like Kisuni!

She asked me another question.

"She wants to know your name," Dad said.

Maybe someday I would adopt Rose as my American name. But not today.

"Jangmi," I replied.

"Jangmi," the girl smiled. "My name is Mary."

"Mary," I smiled back.

I had made a new friend.

Later, when all the guests had gone, I went outside and sat under the maple tree. Dad was right, it *was* beautiful. Maybe someday Mary and I would sit beneath this tree and watch the rain fall. And maybe I would come to love it as much as our willow tree back home in Korea. But not today.

I began to write.

Dear Kisuni...

My best friend was so far away from me. So very, very far. But at least I knew where Kisuni was and what she was doing. She was halfway around the world, sleeping to the sound of a thousand raindrops hitting her clay-tiled roof all at once.

Illustrations are painted in oil on paper.
Book design by Bea Jackson
Text for this book is set in Filosofia. Display text is set in Aspire.

Library of Congress Cataloging-in-Publication Data

Park, Frances, 1955-
Good-bye, 382 Shin Dang Dong / by Frances Park and Ginger Park ;
illustrated by Yangsook Choi.
p. cm.
Summary: Jangmi finds it hard to say goodbye to relatives and friends, plus the food, customs,
and beautiful things of her home in Korea, when her family moves to America.
ISBN 0-7922-7985-9 (Hardcover)
[1. Moving, Household--Fiction. 2. Korea--Fiction. 3. Korean Americans--Fiction.]
I. Title: Good-bye, three eighty two Shin Dang Dong. II. Park, Ginger. III. Choi, Yangsook, ill. IV. Title.
PZ7.P21977 Go 2002
[Fic]--dc21
2001002976

One of the world's largest nonprofit scientific and educational organizations, the National Geographic
Society was founded in 1888 "for the increase and diffusion of geographic knowledge." Fulfilling this
mission, the Society educates and inspires millions every day through its magazines, books, television
programs, videos, maps and atlases, research grants, the National Geographic Bee, teacher workshops, and
innovative classroom materials. The Society is supported through membership dues, charitable gifts, and
income from the sale of its educational products. This support is vital to National Geographic's mission to increase
global understanding and promote conservation of our planet through exploration, research, and education.

NATIONAL GEOGRAPHIC SOCIETY
1145 17th Street N.W.
Washington, D.C. 20036-4688
U.S.A.
Visit the Society's Web site: www.nationalgeographic.com
Printed in the United States of America